CS RICHARDSON has worked as an award-winning book designer for over twenty years. *The End of the Alphabet* is his first novel and is being published in eleven different languages world wide. He is currently at work on his second novel.

FROM THE INTERNATIONAL REVIEWS OF
The End of the Alphabet

'An elegant little fable, charmingly written, and a tender, grateful paean to time, love and literature.' *Guardian*

'Above all else this is a story about love, something longer than the alphabet and wider than geography. This elegant, spare and beautifully written tale of Ambrose Zephyr's last journey is too delicate, witty and passionate to be ruled by alphabetical order or contained within any planned itinerary. The surprise of this little book is not that it is poignant but that it is delightful: graceful, stylish, humorous, intelligent and lacking even the faintest whiff of sanctimony. Each page shimmers with life at its gentle, everyday best: always unravelling at one end of the alphabet or the other, laced with love.' *Washington Post*

'A quirky, feel-good novella.' *Scotland on Sunday*

'*The End of the Alphabet* is a lovely little novel that packs a big emotional wallop. E. B. White, who urged all writers to "omit needless words", would be smitten. The writing is as witty and pointed as the best of Noel Coward's plays. The novel opens and closes with the same line: "This story is unlikely". But aren't the best love stories always unlikely and improbable? *The End of the Alphabet* easily can be read in one sitting. As soon as I finished it, I called my wife to invite her to an impromptu lunch. It's that kind of book.' *USA Today*

'An appealing book [with] a genuine and tender heart.' *FT magazine*

'A sad and sweet debut, with prose as taut as a spider's web. Richardson is a book designer by trade, and the A-to-Z theme, from the characters' names to their lettered journey, reflects it. His love of the 26 building blocks that prop up the entire English language bleeds into the text. Letters have heft and dash and vigour. They lurk as plot points in antique stores and serve up visual trills in alliteration. They turn the pages of this book into a tear-stained goodbye note and a heartfelt love letter.' *L A Times*

'An alphabet of the language of lovers, a beautiful fable of art and morality: elegant, wise and humane.' *Chris Cleave*, author of *Incendiary*

'A gem of a book . . . like a bouquet of roses, beauty in this elegant and witty tale is barbed . . . . This is a very difficult book to put down at bedtime, even when the final page is turned. Richardson not only has an interesting story to tell, but writes with such visual and emotional clarity that the end of one reading readily becomes the start of another.' *Globe and Mail*

'What would you do if you only had 30 days to live? Ambrose Zephyr takes his wife, Zipper, on a beautifully written alpha-betical journey, at the same time taking us on a loving adventure that is both humorous and intense. This is one of the best books I have ever read. I can't get it out of my head.' *Booksense Picks and Notables*

'A journey, crammed with passion and pain, experience and reminiscence, sketches and insight. Simply beautiful.' *The Dominion Post* (New Zealand)

'Funny, sad and intelligent.' *New Books*

'*The End of the Alphabet* is a dazzling exercise in understate-ment. Richardson offers a compelling look at an enviable marriage – one that just happens to be coming to an end.' *People Magazine*

The End of the Alphabet

CS RICHARDSON

BOOKS

First published by Portobello Books Ltd 2008
This paperback edition published 2009

Portobello Books Ltd
Twelve Addison Avenue
Holland Park
London
W11 4QR, UK

A CIP catalogue record is available from the British Library

2 4 6 8 9 7 5 3 1

ISBN 978 1 84627 111 3

www.portobellobooks.com

Printed in the UK by CPI Bookmarque, Croydon, CR0 4TD

Mixed Sources
Product group from well-managed
forests and other controlled sources
www.fsc.org Cert no. TT-COC-002227
© 1996 Forest Stewardship Council
FSC

For Rebecca . . .

TMD

Think of the long trip home

Should we have stayed at home and thought of here?

Where should we be today?

ELIZABETH BISHOP, 'Questions of Travel'

The End of the Alphabet

~

This story is unlikely.

Were it otherwise, or at the least more wished for, it would have begun on a Sunday morning. Early, as that was his best time of the day, and in April, that odd time between a thin winter and a plump spring.

He would have closed the door of his house and stood on his front step, eyeing the predawn sky. He would have given the neighbourhood stray a shove from its perch on his window ledge. The scruffy cat would have hissed and bolted across the narrow road to the park across the way. He would have hissed back, proud he had at last defeated the mangy beast, and set off. As he had every Sunday morning as far back as he could remember.

As he walked up the road, the woman from number eighteen would be retrieving the morning paper from her doorstep. The cool morning would have meant she had remembered to throw on a dressing gown. They would have traded pleasant, awkward good-mornings. He knew her to be the mother of two energetic children whose names he could never recall. She knew he worked in some sort of creative field. After a moment or two of searching for common ground, he would have asked after her children's artwork. He and his wife had no children of their own.

Farther on, he would have seen the elderly man and his tiny dog that lived at number twelve, about to begin their morning walk around the park. The pair would be waiting to say hello. The man would have tipped his cap and launched directly into an eccentric opinion about something. The tiny dog would have begun yapping at the neighbourhood stray.

He would have worried about disagreeing with the old fellow and causing offence, or starting a discussion on a topic he knew nothing about, or the soundness of his own opinion. He would have forced an agreeing laugh, wished his neighbour a good day and eyed the dog with suspicion.

He would have made his way to Kensington High Street and grumbled about the winter that had passed. He would have wished he had taken his wife to Italy. But that would have been expensive or difficult or meant a bad time at the office. He would have sighed to himself, then smiled as the London sky inched from black to grey to yellow to blue.

He would have turned in at Kensington Gardens, up past the palace and on to Broad Walk. Here he would have been happiest. He would have paused near the Round Pond, looked towards the east and the swans, and squinted in his way to watch a girl of perhaps nine or ten, her hair dark and fine and in need of a trim or a ribbon, reading a book beyond her years. He would have closed his eyes in the warmth of a sun just clearing the budding treetops.

He would have checked his watch, counted his minutes and the day's schedule in his head, and turned for home. He would have retraced his route down the Walk, past the palace, along the High Street, into his road, past number twelve and number eighteen and the cat now back on the window ledge, and through his front door.

His wife would have begun to stir in her sleep. Five minutes more, she would have mumbled, just loud enough for him to hear as he made her tea. As usual, a tepid cup with too much milk.

Ambrose Zephyr would have been content that it was Sunday and that spring had come again to that part of London and that there was no need to go to the office. He would have read a draft of his wife's latest magazine column and (as gentle readers are obliged) made one or two enthusiastic comments.

He would have wondered about the days ahead of him and, as was his habit, dreamed of doing something else. And there it would have ended.

But that is not this story.

~

On or about his fiftieth birthday, Ambrose Zephyr failed his annual medical exam. An illness of inexplicable origin with neither known nor foreseeable cure was discovered. It would kill him within the month. Give or take a day.

It was suggested he might want to make arrangements concerning his remaining time.

Ambrose Zephyr lived with his wife—content, quiet, with few extravagances—in a narrow Victorian terrace full of books.

He owned two bespoke suits, one of which he had been married in. The other—a three-piece linen number with lapelled waistcoat—he wore whenever and wherever he travelled: on business, on the underground, on his Sunday walk. A pocket square, discreetly puffed, always in place. He collected French-cuffed shirts as others might collect souvenir spoons or back issues of *National Geographic*. He rarely wore ties but liked them as challenges in graphic design. His footwear was predominantly Italian, loaferish and bought in the sales on Oxford Street. His watches—of which there were many—were a range of silly colours and eccentric shapes.

When cornered, he claimed to read Joyce, Ford and Conrad. Rereads of Fleming and Wodehouse were a more accurate library. His opinion of Miss Elizabeth Bennet was not favourable (though he liked Mr B and held a wary respect for Darcy). *Wuthering Heights*, according to Ambrose, was the dullest book ever written.

He had not read a newspaper in some time.

Everything Ambrose Zephyr knew about cuisine he learned from his wife. He was allowed in the kitchen, but under no circumstance was he to touch anything. He was a courageous eater, save Brussels sprouts and clams. His knowledge of wine was vague and best defined as Napa good, Australian better, French better still. Kir royale was his drink of occasion. For an Englishman, he made a poor cup of tea.

He believed women to be quantifiably wiser than men. He was neither a breast nor a leg nor an ass man; hair could be any length, any colour. Ambrose preferred the complete puzzle to a bit here, a piece there.

He stood when someone entered the room. He walked to the street side. Opened his wife's door first. He could be trusted.

Ambrose Zephyr worked as the creative wallah for Dravot, Carnehan. Ill-mannered competitors termed it the D&C. Messrs Dravot and Carnehan had long ago divested their interests in the advertising agency to a globalizing media concern. The principals then went off to seek other fortunes and left Ambrose working for a wise and exhausted woman named Greta.

Co-workers considered Ambrose to possess an inventive if journeyman approach to the creative process: on time, on budget, realistic, reasonable. He was neither star nor guru. Ambrose was comfortable with that. A client is in the business of selling something, he often said, but that something is usually not Ambrose Zephyr.

—

With his heels to the wall Ambrose stood an inch or two under six feet. Excluding the inevitable middle-years-droop of waist and waddle, his frame was thinnish. His head, well seasoned, carried the same amount of hair it did when he was a boy. His eyes were creased at the corners and as blue as the day when, fifty years before, a young and sad Queen had come home from Africa.

Those who knew him described Ambrose Zephyr as a better man than some. Wanting a few minor adjustments, they would admit, but didn't we all. His wife described him as the only man she had loved. Without adjustment.

Indeed, said the doctor. Arrangements.

Ambrose Zephyr suggested, for all in the outer office to hear, that the doctor might want to wait one damn minute before suggesting that Ambrose might want to arrange his remaining days. Days that until moments before had been assumed would stretch to years. With luck to decades. Not shrink to weeks.

If that, said the doctor.

The room filled with fog. The doctor became a blurry lump behind the desk. The air turned as thick as custard, sauna hot. Ambrose struggled to keep his questions from spilling out with his breakfast in a puddle on the floor.

Something of a mystery, answered the doctor. Not contagious as far as we can tell.

Fatal? Yes, quite.

Very sure.

~

Ambrose Zephyr was married to Zappora Ashkenazi, a woman as comfortable in her own skin as anyone else. She had kept her name for the apparent reasons, would have preferred to have been born a Frenchwoman, suffered fools with grace and a smile, loathed insects.

She had decorated the Victorian terrace in tastefully Swedish DIY, updating as budget and wear dictated. She was resigned to the likelihood that a *pied-à-terre* in the sixth arrondissement might not be in her future. She was content with that.

She wore the best labels she could afford and knew the mysteries that moved a £500 ensemble to the £50 rack. Red and black and white were her 'colours.' Accessorizing she considered well worth the effort, and her earrings were almost always perfect with that outfit. She owned one pair of stilettoed shoes that hurt just to look at. But Ambrose liked them. Which was enough.

She read everything. Russian epics, French confections, American noir, English tabloids had at one time or another taken their place in a wobbly pile beside the bed. Non-fiction was too much like school, she said. Experimental literature left her cold and annoyed and despairing for the so-called modern craft. She had lost count of how many times she had read *Wuthering Heights*.

She could walk into a kitchen she had never seen before and—without a recipe—plate a meal worthy of a starred review in half the time it took her husband to find an egg to boil. Her kitchen was full of cookery books that had never felt the splash of an errant sauce. She read them, she displayed them; they felt good in hand. They completed the room. Like earrings.

Men brought out her best and made her laugh. She liked most beards, hated all moustaches and furrowed her brow at the mention of tattoos. Height and weight and size didn't matter. Manners and nice shoes mattered. Doing the better thing mattered.

Her shoulder was ready when friends felt a cry coming on. She knew where to offer opinion and when to shut up. She could juggle oranges. She lied only a little, and they were always white.

Zappora Ashkenazi was the literary editor for the country's third most-read fashion magazine. Her publisher had wanted to introduce the magazine's reluctant readership to both new and classic literature, and if that literature held a passing link to couture, so much the better. It was a job with challenge: Austen, Woolf and Parker had never, so far as Zappora knew, assembled a spring collection. Yet those who read 'On the Night Stand' every month did so faithfully and first. Her writing was known for its economic style and refreshing avoidance of simile. Her husband was her first reader. Every word, every draft. You always have an interesting story to tell, he would say.

Zappora started in the fashion trade as a photographer's dresser. She flipped collars, fanned skirts, hitched pants, buttoned, tied, zipped. By the end of the first hour with her first model on her first day of her first real job she was given her first nickname.

Zipper.

She was very proud.

Zipper was not quite as tall as her husband, not quite as thin and not quite as old. Her hair was dark and fine and trimmed precisely every eight weeks. Coloured, perhaps tied with a ribbon, as required.

Her eyes were creased at the corners. She wore

glasses when reading. The glasses were purchased in a small shop in Paris, around the corner from an antiquarian bookshop.

~

Zipper sat silent beside her husband, thinking how curious it was that her body had stopped working. That the doctor sounded like he was speaking under water.

She wondered what would happen if she got up and left. Better yet, hadn't come in at all. She clung to the sense of it.

I am not in the room.

Ambrose is not unravelling into the sweating, pasty stranger sitting next to me.

We are at home, preparing a meal for friends or

deciding which film to see or selecting which book to curl up with or standing on the doorstep watching that annoying cat with those stupid birds.

We are not here.

None of this is happening to us.

~

Depending on the storyteller, Ambrose and Zipper met for the first or second time in the offices of Dravot, Carnehan. The third most-read fashion magazine in the country was at the time a fledgling and unread concept. It was being pitched to the city's advertising community in an effort to change that.

Messrs Dravot and Carnehan sat at one end of their unnecessarily long boardroom table. Ambrose stood in a corner trying to look creative. He was the only man in the room not wearing a tie. The magazine's presentation team was led by a painfully loud publisher and trailed by a nervous junior editor, introduced as Young Ms Ashkenazi Who I Believe Will Be Heading Up Our Literary Efforts.

Ambrose would later admit to a nagging sensation of having seen this Ms Ashkenazi before. How he could not place her, but that her handshake felt small, warm, a touch damp. How he could not take his eyes off her. And how, more than once, he had narrowed his gaze to watch her, topless, eating tapas on a beach in Spain. She might have been twenty, maybe twenty-one years old. It was hard to see clearly, Ambrose would explain, what with the sun and the heat and the glare off the sea.

Zipper had an equally odd feeling throughout the meeting. She thought, but couldn't be sure, that she knew the slightly handsome man in the corner who said nothing. (What she never mentioned to anyone was the pleasant hum she felt as Ambrose spent the meeting trying not to glance at her breasts. Or that she found his periodic squint boyishly charming.)

Looking back, Ambrose and Zipper agreed the

meeting could not have ended soon enough. As we'll-be-in-touch's went around the room, Ambrose complimented Ms Ashkenazi on her glasses. In that moment Zipper recalled where she had seen this man before.

Coffee? Ambrose then suggested.

It's Zappora. Zipper, actually.

But if you'd rather not . . .

Zipper smiled.

You're busy then . . . not to worry. Right. *Zipper*? Well. Yes. Lovely. Perhaps another time . . . Have we met? No, my mistake. There you are. Sorry. Right. Well.

Zipper remembered the rain in Paris. Tea would be brilliant, she said.

Ambrose escorted the magazine team to the street. While everyone waited for taxis and compared notes for their next presentation, Zipper conjured a case of performance nerves and told the team she'd catch up. Ambrose never went back to the office.

They spent the rest of the morning and the better

part of the afternoon in a tiny café near Seven Dials. The next day a grinning Ambrose turned up at D&C at noon, wearing a shambled version of the clothes he had worn the day before.

Ambrose Zephyr later claimed that Zipper was the only woman he had ever been honest with. Not that he had ever misled anyone (perhaps a mild fib here and there), but with Zipper there would be no showing off, no blurring of unfortunate detail, no exaggeration for effect. In the face of all reason she was interested in him as he was. Not as he wished he was.

From that morning across the boardroom table, or earlier—depending on the storyteller—on a narrow street in Paris, Ambrose and Zipper were almost effortless.

They were married beside an anonymous willow near a statue of Peter Pan.

It was a small, drenched affair. All parents

attended, as uncomfortable as newly met in-laws can be, but managing to find common ground in grumbles about the weather, the venue, the damned informality of it all. A blown light bulb from the recently acquired and completely bare Victorian terrace was broken under foot.

The following week a notice ran in the social pages of the Sunday editions:

ZEPHYR/ASHKENAZI. Saturday last, at Kensington Gardens. Ambrose Zephyr (Esq) and Zappora Ashkenazi (Ms), attended by Katerina Mankowitz (Ms) of Bayswater and Frederick Wilkes (Esq) of Her Majesty's Foreign Office. The bride, who will retain her maiden name, wore a vintage ensemble in off-white, tailored by Umtata's of Old Jewry. The couple is currently honeymooning on the continent. Their long-term plans were not available at press time.

Why you? Why anyone? responded the doctor.

I'm afraid not. Nothing to be done.

Unlikely, but perhaps.

Could be, but doubtful.

How long? Thirty days. Give or take.

Faculties may dull a bit. Blurred eyesight, ringing ears, numbed fingertips. That sort of thing. Happens rather quickly as far as we can tell.

Yes, the doctor offered, unfair would be a very good word about now.

Ambrose Zephyr's father toiled as a wordsmith for one of the more popular broadsheets of the day. Not long after writing his son's wedding notice, he had taken an early retirement. Enough reading about it, he told his wife.

Mr Zephyr died five days later. His heart had stopped as he walked to the corner shop for milk and the day's papers. There was no good reason, said the coroner.

Ambrose's mother called her son at the offices of D&C. When Ambrose rang off, he threw his collection of antique type blocks across the room. They shattered the window separating him from the creative department. He sat there, surrounded by bits of glass and stared at by the younger talents in the office, for most of the morning.

In the months that followed, Mrs Zephyr took to calling her son at all hours, moaning about this ache or that pain. She began complaining about her tea, convinced someone had changed the mixture after two hundred years and how dare the bastards. She whined about the Queen.

On the good days Ambrose would offer, as pleasantly as he could, to take his mother to the National Gallery. Too crowded, she said. What's on the telly? Not *that* tea.

One Sunday afternoon, Ambrose stopped by for a visit. He found his mother sitting on the floor in her kitchen, surrounded by a week's worth of newspapers, whimpering at the mess around her.

I can't remember his face, she said.

A neighbour called Ambrose the next day to

say his mother had passed quietly in her sleep. That evening, for the first time since he was old enough to read, Ambrose Zephyr did not look at a newspaper. There were other things happening in the world.

~

Ambrose Zephyr sat dumb and frozen on his front step. He may have seen something like the elderly man from number twelve carrying his tiny dog around the park. Or number eighteen returning from work, her children bouncing on the pavement and brandishing their day's art. Or the neighbourhood stray rousing from its spot on the window ledge and strolling defiantly towards the birds.

Ambrose and Zipper made something like love that night. It was rough, frantic, tearful, quick. Ambrose rolled away and went downstairs without saying a word. Zipper lay perfectly still, staring at the ceiling. Tears trickled into her ears. She thought she could hear her husband shaking in the dark.

Ambrose Zephyr began life a loved if overshadowed baby. Mrs Zephyr's labour started while she was listening to the radio: the King was dead and his daughter, now a young and sad Queen, was returning from Kenya. Mr Zephyr was delayed at the office—a new Queen did not come along every day—and could not meet his son until the special edition had started coming off the presses.

—

Not so many years later, on a Saturday evening,

Mr Zephyr took young Ambrose to the newspaper's offices. He showed his son the collection of retired wood and lead typefaces on display in the lobby. Young Ambrose liked the way the small type blocks felt large and heavy in his hand. He liked the tidy way each type was organized—one letter, one cubby —in a large flat wooden drawer. At the same time, he was angry that Z lived in such a small space compared to A. It isn't fair, he said with a dark scowl.

His father tut-tutted. Such is the manner of alphabets, he said. Some types are luckier than others. A may have more space in the drawer, but Z is no less important, particularly when it comes to words like zebra.

Or Zephyr, said Ambrose, straightening his small back.

Or Zanzibar, said his father. A place very far away.

A place with *two* z's?

Indeed. And two a's.

I think I would like that place, said Ambrose.

Mrs Zephyr worked as a junior art appraiser for a large and prestigious auction house. The art she usually appraised was neither. When her son was eight or perhaps nine she took him on his first visit to the National Gallery. To see the proper stuff, she said.

She explained all that they saw: who the artist was, where the painting had come from, how old or new it was, who the people on the canvases were. Ambrose found some of the paintings boring, particularly those with snobby children in satin suits and silly collars. He liked the paintings that featured a lot of blood. Or people dying. This preference he kept from his mother.

Ambrose also noticed quite a few paintings of naked women. Lying on beds, wrestling with naked men, holding haloed babies, admiring themselves in mirrors. Ambrose wondered whether artists ever got erections as they painted these women. This question he also kept from his mother.

When Mrs Zephyr started talking about the *school* of this or the *ism* of that, Ambrose stopped listening.

To him what he saw was what it was. Some paintings made him wonder, some made him giggle, some made him squirm. The Dutch Master with his floppy clown hat and thin beard and bright eyes, the chubby girls with their chubby dogs, the giant sunflowers drooping out of their pot like alien plant people with one bulging green eye.

. . . painted by a troubled young man, Mrs Zephyr was saying, . . . cut off part of his own ear . . .

Ambrose went back to looking. What he saw didn't need his mother going on about symbols and meanings and madness and genius, he thought. She knew a lot, but she didn't know when to stop complicating things. The sunflowers were like none he had ever seen, ear or no ear, troubles or not.

Ambrose Zephyr liked what he liked and didn't like what he didn't like.

It was as simple as that.

Zipper woke to what felt like something heavy being dragged from under her, mingled with the sound of her husband's whispers.

Must go now . . . leave today . . . no time . . . no waiting . . . arrangements . . . places to be . . . a list . . . A is for . . .

Ambrose was naked. Sweat dripped off him as he rummaged under the bed. The large suitcase snagged on the bedsprings. He pulled it free and in the same motion threw it on the bed.

Austria? . . . no . . . B for Belize? . . . no . . . people

to see . . . things must be done . . . make a list . . .
have a plan . . . go now . . . C is for . . .

It was a square and handsome case: oxblood
leather, reinforced corners, brass hinges. A thick
handle. A man's handle. It looked like it had never
been used for anything other than storage.

As a boy, Ambrose Zephyr was considered by the neighbours to be well mannered, agreeable and quiet. *Average* was a word often used. That is, they said, aside from the travel brochures. And the alphabets.

He spent days alone in his room, compiling addresses for every embassy, mission and consulate in London. He wrote letters, in his best hand, to each ambassador or commissioner or consul explaining that he was planning to visit their country in the very near future and would Sir or Madam be so kind as to possibly forward any and all information concerning their fine country at the earliest possible convenience yours very sincerely Master Ambrose Zephyr Esq. He worked for hours perfecting the proper amount of swoosh to his Z's.

On one wall of his room he had taped a large map (which the Prime Minister's office had forwarded after Ambrose had enquired about the nations of the Commonwealth and was there, Mr Prime Minister, Sir, a particular reason why each was shaded pink). Ambrose stuck redheaded pins in the places that replied with the glossiest literature. Within a few weeks, Switzerland became a small red hedgehog popping from the top of an Italian boot.

When he wasn't corresponding with dignitaries, Ambrose Zephyr was drawing. A's through Z's. In the hundreds. Twenty-six at a time, plus punctuation, numerals and ampersands.

Some of his alphabets were illustrated with less popular members of the animal world: *A is for anaconda, B is for booby, C is for codfish.* Some depicted the world on his map: *D is for a Beach in the Dutch Antilles, E is for the Windy Coast of Elba, F is for Palm Trees in Florida.* Some combined the two themes: *G is for Geckos in the German Woods, H is for Hellenic Capybaras in a Taverna, I is for Italian Bats in the Vatican Belfry.* When his father asked why A wasn't apple or B wasn't bird or C wasn't cat, young Ambrose explained that things didn't always have to be the way you'd expect.

Everybody does apples and birds and cats, he said, and it's boring to do what everybody else does and I'm not much good at drawing cats anyway I can never get the feet right.

~

A list of what? said Zipper.

. . . Calcutta . . . sorry? whispered Ambrose. List?
Yes. What?

Come back to bed.

Places . . . things . . .

What things?

Places . . . A is for . . .

Zipper pulled the duvet and her knees to her chin
and watched her husband empty the suitcase. Scores
of brochures, advertisements, maps, booklets, supplements, catalogues and flyers spilled onto the bed.

Together with hundreds of drawings: some childish and faded, others by a more accomplished hand. All of them letters. A through Z. Everything formed a small mountain on the bed and spilled onto the floor.

Where? said Zipper.

Things, said Ambrose.

Like?

Places. A to Z equals twenty-six. A month equals thirty. The doctor said as much. Or is it twenty-nine? What year is this? Twenty-eight? A month, give or take.

I know what the doctor said. Are you all right?

Fine.

Then come back to bed.

What would you do?

What?

DO. What. Would. You. Do.

About what?

Time, time, time. Thirty days. No time. Weren't you listening?

Don't ask me that.

———

Tea came and went as Zipper reviewed her husband's list. *Places . . . Things.* 1) *A is for a Portrait in Amsterdam.* . . . There was no mention of putting affairs in order, no alternative remedies, no sprinkling of ashes under an anonymous willow in Kensington Gardens. Zipper's mind spun. This was not her Ambrose, she thought at first. But then, apparently, it was.

Paris being so far down the list and what happened after Zanzibar and why was X blank and how and what with and what if and are you mad and should we and shouldn't we and how could you and don't do this don't be this don't go without me don't go at all were thoughts Zipper fought to keep down.

Instead, she frowned and suggested that Andalusia might be nicer this time of year.

Habitually (in blind panic, she would later admit), Zipper edited. She pencilled a stroke through Valparaiso, a place she had never heard of, and in the margin wrote *Venice*.

The love they made that morning was tender, lingering and generous. She before he.

After, they talked of the Bridge of Sighs.

A

The ferry from Harwich crossed a rough and cold sea. The passage did not agree with Zipper and she spent most of it below decks. Ambrose, waved off for useless hovering, spent most of it at the railing watching the lights along the European shore grow brighter on the horizon. They ate lunch the next day in a café at the edge of a pretty square in Amsterdam.

Ambrose was dressed in his linen travel number: hastily pressed, pocket-squared. Zipper in a white cotton blouse and black trousers cut in a capri style. Ambrose had always admired the way her back moved in that outfit. Her shoes were comfortable. Red.

Amidst sips of coffee and suggested itineraries, Zipper remembered a conversation.

Lovely, she said.

Sorry. What? Ambrose said.

The Velázquez.

Sorry? Yes.

They had been married most of a year. Having coaxed Ambrose into taking her on one of his usually solitary visits to the National Gallery, Zipper had done some reading beforehand.

Venus at Her Mirror, Zipper said.

The Rockeby Venus, said Ambrose.

The model was somebody's mistress?

The king of Spain. Philip, I think.

Had a thing for black taffeta sheets.

The king?

The mistress. And didn't a suffragette attack her with a knife?

The mistress?

The painting. Are you listening?

Right. Yes.

It's the sheets, Zipper said. They highlight the form. Her form. And Velázquez painted her hazy reflection in the mirror on purpose. Forces the eye to the form. Sorry, *her* form. Critics said the reflection looked un-finished. The optics were wrong. We should be seeing her torso reflected in the mirror. How am I doing?

Sorry. Yes. Lovely.

What, precisely, is so lovely?

Her. This. The Velázquez.

Why?

Because it is.

That's it?

I think so. Yes.

You're impossible, Zipper said. All I know is what I've read. All I'd like to know is what *you* know. What *you* think.

About what?

About *why*, damn it. Why the sheets and the

optics and the mistress and the unfinished reflection? Why love it so much? Why her?

It is what it is, said Ambrose. Lovely.

You're exhausting.

Fine. If you insist, it reminds me of you.

Really. My backside is not nearly so lovely.

I wasn't looking at her backside.

Really.

I was looking at her front. The slope of the neck. Curve of the breasts, the smooth stomach. The gentle hollow around the navel. Her face.

You're imagining things.

Isn't that the point?

They thought better of visiting the Rijksmuseum together.

Zipper said she wasn't sure how she would spend the day. Ambrose did his best to reassure. There was, he said, no need to worry. They kissed and Ambrose set off to find a portrait he had seen before. But long ago and from very far away.

A younger Ambrose arrived behind his time, having spent most of the previous day in the pub with Freddie Wilkes.

It was the oldest lecture theatre on campus: a cavernous circular space with graceful plasterwork, smelling of mould and varnish and nervous sweat. The few windows it had were small, painted forever shut, and set high behind tiers of hard benches worn by a century or two of first-term buttocks.

Ambrose found a seat in the back rows and consulted his schedule. *The Place of the Portrait.* Below him the professor paced the dais, a small man gesturing with a long pointer at his latest slide: a Rembrandt, late in the artist's career. The reproduction was poor. The slide was scratched from years of projection, the contrast blown, the detail flattened to blobs.

It was a group portrait. *The Company of Captain Frans Banning Cocq and Lieutenant Willem van Ruytenburch*, announced the professor. Painted in 1642. You may, if you must, call it *The Night Watch.*

Captain Cocq's company—by the professor's pointed count—consisted of thirty-five adults, two children, one chicken and one dog, as well as various lances, spears, pikes, walking canes, drums, flags and muskets.

The professor rambled at length about dynamic magnetism and profound insight and asymmetric composition. NOTE IF YOU WILL, he kept yelling . . . the significance of this . . . symbolism of that . . . transcendence of genre . . . portrait of genius . . .

Ambrose raised his thick head and stared at the projection. Not once had the professor mentioned a shadowed half-face, hardly visible behind the painted crowd, peeking back at Ambrose with a pair of bright and smiling eyes.

In a grand and old department store Zipper wandered from floor to floor. Here a blouse held to her chest and re-hung on its rack; there the silk of a scarf, fingered and left folded. She sampled a lipstick that matched, precisely, the colour of her shoes.

Assistants asked if madame required help. Zipper felt her eyes water and managed no thank you. She left the store without buying anything.

She came across a small bookshop in a tilted narrow building. A sign in the window advertised Gently Read Literature, Items for Composition and Correspondence Within. Zipper shuffled around the shop, finally settling on a small leather journal, rounded at the corners. An envelope for keeping reminders and receipts and bits of things was bound inside the back cover, a thick elastic band held all in place. The proprietor was still counting change as Zipper ran out of the shop.

She struggled to catch her breath, needed to sit down, went cold, thought she was going to vomit. She found a bench overlooking a canal and sat on her hands to hide the tremors. She stared at a passing tourist barge, her eyes filling with panic as those on board practised ducking under footbridges yet to come.

The shaking stopped as suddenly as it had begun.

Zipper had nothing to wipe her eyes. Flustered, she used the sleeve of her blouse. She stood, unsure of her knees, and headed off to meet her husband at the train station.

Ambrose Zephyr reviewed the departures board, confirmed the overnight train would be leaving on time and made his way to the platform to meet his wife. If someone were no wiser, he might have looked as content as a man on holiday.

Zipper watched her husband approach. Relieved at his relaxed way, she closed her journal. A souvenir postcard—a garish reproduction of a group portrait by Rembrandt—peeked from the envelope inside the cover. Ambrose paid no attention. He was too busy telling his story.

. . . bigger than I expected. Enormous. More like a company of giants . . . There he was, behind the watchmen, the children, the chicken, the dog, the lances and spears and pikes and canes, the drums, the flags, the muskets . . . the master himself, peeking over a shoulder with those laughing eyes, I swear they winked . . .

Ambrose flailed and paced like an awkward conductor.

. . . and sweep and swirl and banners and action and such a good Rembrandt and luscious and bold and warm and thick with amazing outfits . . . the lieutenant in yellow of all things . . .

Ambrose caught his breath.

. . . and the genius?

Zipper ventured a guess. His use of light?

Work for hire, said Ambrose. Commissioned and paid for by the Captain et al. Hah! *There's* your genius. There's the art.

Zipper smiled. Until then, she had always assumed the Rembrandt was what it was.

On the night train to Berlin, Ambrose slept as well as anyone sitting upright on a train might. Zipper sat clutching the journal until her hands went clammy. She tried opening it a few times. A thousand words flew through her head but she couldn't manage to land any on the page.

After a while she gave up and watched the dark grey countryside speed past her reflection in the window.

B

They sat at an outdoor table on the Unter den Linden. The sky was clear, blue, welcoming. The lime trees showed an early-spring green and offered comfortable shade.

Nearby stood a brooding Brandenburg Gate, all heavy stone and column. Tourists and locals and friends and lovers were enjoying the morning, strolling through the gate as if it wasn't there.

Zipper Ashkenazi's legs stretched from under her, her shoes off. She watched a street entertainer prepare for the day's performance: unfolding a music stand, tuning a battered violin. She had passed a poor night, but on this morning and in this place she was content.

Ambrose stewed. He knew he needed to be here. He knew he needed to get past this. He knew it would make Zipper happy. But still he fussed and squirmed in search of a comfortable place in his chair. He kept an eye on the gate and scowled.

He claimed he was only thinking of his uncle, but Zipper knew there was more to it than that.

At one time or another, Ambrose had spoken of his Uncle Jack. How he had taught an annoyingly inquisitive nephew the subtleties of life. The first gentleman I ever met, Ambrose would say.

Every Remembrance Sunday, Jack came up to the city, wearing the same threadbare jacket and regimental tie he had worn the year before. His shoes always shone, he smelt freshly shaved, he stood whenever Mrs Zephyr entered or left the room. He had an unsure smile that matched his limp.

One particular November young Ambrose asked

his uncle about the war. What had he done? Where had he been?

All over, said Jack. France, Holland, Berlin.

That's right. Germany.

Wasn't very nice.

People weren't very nice either.

Didn't like us, I suppose. They didn't like a lot of people.

They did. People they'd no business killing.

Friends? A few.

No. I didn't help my friends. I was away.

A few years later at his uncle's funeral, Ambrose read about someone named Sylvia. She had died when an air raid blew up her house near Spitalfields. Jack had left her a note, apologizing for not being there. For not keeping her safe.

Zipper knew that, with odd exception, Ambrose held a modern view of the world. He kept himself informed well enough, knew there was neither black nor white, believed what the BBC told him. Yet when she reminisced about her younger location-shoot days in Germany, she could watch his view become as black and blind as ash. With an unnerving Berlin at its centre.

In its greyness. The weather always threatening, the streets always wet. The architecture all cold stone: large and hard and lacking in windows.

With its inhabitants. Sour and stiff with permanently furrowed expressions. They spoke a jarring language: phlegmy, incapable of expressions of love. No one smiled. Laughter was faked. There never seemed to be any children.

With its music. Unlistenable. Funereal. Loud.

And its ghosts. Prowling, wearing uniforms, black, brown, grey. Lurking in doorways, dropping bombs on houses, burning Zipper's books. Watching and waiting to steal her away.

That was then, Zipper said. Jack was then.

She pulled Ambrose to his feet and they set off to walk the city she knew.

They made their way through the Reichstag. Once an asylum run by madmen, now through its centre an atrium of glass and mirror poured sky into the building and warmed Ambrose's upturned face.

They visited the zoo, where people had once eaten the animals left behind. On this day it was full of children, laughing at the monkeys, waving at the pandas, having their photographs taken by tired parents.

Along more than one boulevard Ambrose and Zipper jostled past crowded coffee bars and neon dance clubs and persistent gypsy beggars; bored fashion models and charged young lovers and old people with old dogs; graffiti artists and boisterous hawkers and women for sale and men who smiled like cartoon spies and made Ambrose chuckle.

They walked, perhaps a little lost, along Oranienburgerstrasse and through an ancient neighbourhood. They asked directions from a young man with a long and unkempt beard. He mumbled through his whiskers and pointed vaguely down the street. Zipper thanked him in the only Yiddish she could recall. The man grinned and shuffled Ambrose and Zipper along their way.

As dusk came, they returned to the avenue under the lime trees. The street performer was calling for last requests. Ambrose watched a woman in tailored red trousers and a black turtleneck approach the violinist. She whispered in his ear. The performer bowed and played the opening notes of the woman's request. She turned to her companion, a reluctant gentleman with greying hair, and offered her hand. The couple danced to a waltz composed by a German whose name Ambrose could not recall.

This is now, Zipper said, as she picked up a small stone and slid it in her pocket. The sky grew dark and the stars came out.

Ambrose smiled and asked if she had said something. If she was safe. If she was happy.

C

As the high-speed train crossed into France, its vending machines served Ambrose Zephyr a breakfast of stale croissant and muddy coffee. He checked his watch, took a measure of the fields whizzing past the window, and announced to his wife that an improved lunch would, with luck, be served in Chartres.

Zipper declined breakfast for the apparent reasons. In silence she fretted over maths: days spent, days remaining, days to come. Couldn't we just stay in one place, she thought. *C rhymes with P*. Which stood for Paris. Too many days away.

She tried thinking of clever ways to rearrange the alphabet. Her brain refused the work. Instead she imagined a proper meal and a change of clothes; a nap in a quiet spot near the river, a view of the cathedral. At the least, food or fresh underwear or rest would pass the time while Ambrose attended church.

He was fond of repeatedly telling the story of his best day in advertising. A day, so the story began, when Ambrose Zephyr informed a client that they didn't need any advertising.

The client was a little church in the midst of London. For a hundred years or more, it had served its congregation plainly and true. But times—as are their custom—had changed. The parish had retired to the country and filled itself with a more distracted demographic. Those who worshipped at all were doing so in a score of different ways. The little church had fallen on competitive days.

A young priest was newly arrived in the parish

and, in the way of the young and the new, saw an opportunity to make his mark. To put the arses, he whispered to Ambrose at their first meeting, back in the pews.

Ambrose was vague on church business. As a boy, he had attended Sunday lessons perhaps once or twice that he could recall. He was cinematically familiar with a few biblical stories. But he knew well the first law of his profession: walk in thy client's shoes. A tour of the little church was decided upon.

It stood, small and quiet and tucked away at the end of a noisy lane, surrounded by office blocks of glass and steel and looming business. Inside, three pews sat on either side of the aisle. Each pew held a sprig of fresh flowers. Changed every other day, said the priest with much pride. Whatever the market had in bloom. On this day the nave smelled of lavender.

A simple cross was placed on the altar, itself a plain wooden desk. A round window tucked among the rafters above the altar provided as much sunlight as could find its way between the office towers.

Someone had painted a pastel blue sky on the ceiling. Here and there a cloud. Angels, cherubim, beams of light were nowhere to be found. Around the walls were twelve tiny stained glass windows. Those, boasted the priest, were new.

Ambrose expected the windows to hold the usual scenes, rendered in heavy glass with thick colours and serious overtones. Instead they were as graceful as locket portraits. One depicted a young mother with a pushchair. In another a team of small boys played football. Here was a wedding party. There a lovers' kiss. An old man walking in a park with his dog, a tearful goodbye, a welcome home. The windows were the stations of a life, but the life was anyone's.

Ambrose spent a long time with the young priest's windows, quietly moving around the nave and saying nothing. Finally the priest cleared his throat and broached the subject of professional opinion. Where do we begin? he asked.

A party, answered Ambrose.

A party?

With a bar. Music, all kinds. Food, all kinds. Games for the children. Fun.

A *party*?

Any day but Sunday.

—

Ambrose's story always ended with the dashing of a young priest's hopes. Television time and electronic billboards and colour supplements and celebrity endorsements were not the thing required.

Sandwiches were the thing, Ambrose said. Together with a place where one can rest, gaze up at a blue sky with a few gentle clouds and take a breath. This place, Ambrose declared as he tapped his finger on the seat of a pew, is where the arses will go. Here is all the advertising you need.

A charming story, those who had heard it too often would say, but hardly believable.

Lunch, as promised, was improved. The waiter appeared with dipped madeleines. As madame prefers, he said. Zipper blushed at the discreet nods between her husband and the maître d' as Ambrose left the café. Nibbling at the chocolate, she watched her husband turn in the direction of the cathedral.

Zipper found a ladies' atelier and slipped into a new outfit of black blouse, red silk scarf and white calf-length skirt. She remembered the restorative effects of French clothes. At a flower shop she bought a small bouquet of spring blooms. She walked down a steep cobbled lane and chose a quiet spot by the river with a clear view of the cathedral.

She opened her journal and thought of writing. *E is for Eiffel's tower, standing in Paris. L is for London and home. Z is for Zipper. T is for terrified. H is hopeless.*

The journal remained blank. Shadows lengthened as Zipper made her way up the lane to the cathedral. *L*, she thought, *is for lost.*

The day's crowds had thinned and Ambrose was easy to find. He stood near the middle of the nave, at the centre of a labyrinth inlaid in the stone floor seven hundred years earlier. A few pilgrims traced the labyrinth's penitent paths. Zipper was unnerved by how cold, how dark, how threatening the huge space was.

All around Ambrose were the cathedral's famous windows. Windows that poured blue light into the black and frigid gothic space; that told stories and offered answers and provided comfort; that beckoned locals and pilgrims and tourists, the committed and the curious. And had been doing so long before television and billboards and supplements and celebrity.

Zipper hovered near the door, memorizing the view of her husband gazing around the cathedral whilst old women circled him on their knees. He spun this way and that, not knowing where to look next. He caught sight of Zipper and smiled.

Truly, thought Zipper. It had been one of his best days in advertising.

Nearing midnight, the hum of Zipper Ashkenazi's mobile raised a sweat in the small of her back.

On the line: the publisher of the country's third most-read fashion magazine. A sour-candy woman named Pru. A yeller in the workplace, a screamer on the phone.

WHERE ARE YOU?

The sound of Pru's voice turned Ambrose away from watching Normandy scroll past the train. He checked his watch and cringed sympathetically to his wife.

In France, replied Zipper.

THE ISSUE IS CLOSING. Photo needs another page. Your page? BLANK. *Fave Books of Fab People.* Really, who bloody cares . . . WHERE?

I meant to call.

WORLDS ARE CRASHING, ZIP. Subs down. Ads cancelled. Printer wants for payment. Have you resigned or something?

I should have called.

HOW BLOODY RIGHT YOU ARE. I'm tired of keeping this rag afloat. Sick or something?

I needed some time.

BE MY BLOODY GUEST. Meanwhile, what am I supposed to do?

Give photo the page. I wish I'd called. Honestly. Sorry.

NOT HALF AS BLOODY SORRY, Zip, NOT HALF.

Something came up.

SOMETHING LIKE LEAVING? If you jump I bloody swear . . .

I need a month. Give or take.

NOW IS NOT the time. Ring when you get back.
THE BLOODY SEC—

Zipper closed the phone.

Ambrose borrowed his wife's phone and placed a
call to D&C. Someone would be there. Greta was
always there.

Grets? Ambrose.

France.

I know. Sorry.

Nothing. Something came up.

Sorry, no. I'm not leaving. Not exactly.

It's more personal. I'll explain later.

Yes, I should have called.

The client will be fine. Storyboards done, shoot
booked, talent hired, wardrobe enroute, print ads on
my desk.

Yes, I'm sure. Wrote them myself.

The pitch? You do the pitch.

Can't. Sorry. It should be you anyway. It's your
agency, your client. I'm just the help.

The client does not hate you.

He does *not* hate Germans.

Get the account lads to lend a hand. Threaten the sack. They'll understand that.

I'm okay. Thanks.

How Long? A month. Maybe less. I'll let you know.

You'll do fine in the meantime.

I'll call if I can.

D

On their fourth day from home, Ambrose and Zipper sat in comfortable beach chairs watching the English Channel. It was a bright afternoon, the sun was high, the offshore breeze chilled a day more winter than spring. But for the time gone by and the time of year, they could have been any honeymooning couple.

Despite her squinting and her husband's pointing, Zipper could not see England. Just there, Ambrose kept insisting, jabbing his finger northward. Zipper could see the row of vacant bathing tents stretching along the beach, gaily striped for the coming season. A small girl in blue gumboots playing with a large dog at the water's edge, a calm sea beyond. A few working boats idled in the middle distance; a few heavy ships ploughed the lanes farther out. But there was no far shore in her sight. Past the ships, said Ambrose. At the horizon. *Just there.*

Zipper gave up and lay back in her chair, annoyed. She knew the story. The Curious Talents of Ambrose Zephyr, or, The Business of Seeing Things Just There. To a disinterested listener, it might have been another tired story of the imaginings of children. To Zipper it was a story a concerned parent might quietly slip to his new daughter-in-law, just before he and the missus waved their happy children off to a wedding weekend in Deauville.

According to Mr Zephyr's story, at the age of eleven, perhaps twelve, Ambrose announced to his parents that he possessed a talent. The announcement occurred during the family's annual motoring holiday. They were on the Cornish coast.

I can see better than anything, young Ambrose said.

Any one, said his father.

Better than animals.

That is something, said his mother.

Better than binoculars.

You don't say, said Mr Zephyr.

I do say.

And how did you come by this talent? asked Mrs Zephyr.

Ambrose shrugged.

Indeed, said his father.

Ambrose's face began to glow.

He was standing on the last cliff of England, squinting as boys do, and seeing America. A soft blue lump, right at the horizon. Just there, Ambrose insisted, jabbing his finger westward. The Manhattan skyline emerged through the low ocean mist. His parents apologized for not being able to quite make out the details. They blamed the time of day and the angle of the sun.

Two summers later. On a tour through northern Europe Ambrose asked his mother to stop the car before each border crossing: could he walk the last few metres and stand on the frontier? At one such stop, recalled Mr Zephyr, his son's left foot stood in Belgium, the right in Luxembourg. Ambrose then peered along the line (invisible to the senior Zephyrs) as it crossed the road.

On the same holiday Ambrose also announced he could see the difference between one country's soil and another's. The difference (and the talent to see it) was never defined. There was, young Ambrose said, just . . . something. Denmark was . . . browner, he offered his perplexed parents.

And the air too. From one country to the next, Ambrose could detect a change in the smell of things. Sometimes cleaner, sometimes mustier. France smelt like apples, Germany like freshly cut grass, Holland like wet socks. Ambrose declared he could smell it the moment he stepped over each border. Hopping in and out of Luxembourg, he explained: flowers . . . dogs . . . flowers . . . dogs . . . flowers . . . dogs.

As Zipper and her new in-laws stood on the platform waiting for the groom to return with the cross-Channel tickets, Mr Zephyr's hushed story continued. His son's curious and increasingly annoying talent extended beyond the here-and-now. He could see the past. Events great and significant, faces grand and notorious, battles won and lost. The further back in time the better, apparently. With the proper amount of squint, explained the boy, he could see what had happened or who had walked on the ground where he stood. Ten, a hundred, a thousand years ago.

Young Ambrose offered proof: the time he had emerged from the underground near the Tower of London and there was the Duke of Norfolk's piked and dripping head, as if the Virgin Queen herself had pruned it the day before. Or the summer he saw William the Conqueror wading through the sun-bathers on the Hastings shore. Or the party of Druids he watched at Stonehenge while Mr and Mrs Zephyr read the visitor pamphlets. They were just a work crew, Ambrose assured his parents. Squaring a few lintel stones.

The end of the story came when Mr Zephyr mentioned that he and the missus had once spent a lovely picnic afternoon watching their boy gaze across a flat and empty field in Flanders. He just stood there, said Mr Zephyr. For hours. And I have no doubt, he added with a wink, the boy was in mud to his knees. Ah, here's your train.

Ambrose Zephyr gave up. Can't seem to see it either, he said. He lay back in his chair. After a moment or two of watching a few clouds pass overhead, he told his wife what he remembered.

The bloody queues. Bathing tents, ices, chairs, towels, the loo. Stretched the length of the beach.

We changed in our room. Ran half-naked through the lobby. It took us hours to find a vacant bit of sand. Nasty dogs and noisy children everywhere. The tents were a different colour that year. Were they green? I remember it was too cold to swim. The Channel was rough. First weekend of the season. Windy. Not even the local boats were out. You hated the sand. Yes you did. Insisted on wearing those horrible blue trainers. From the ankle up you were breathtaking. A fantastic bikini, red I think. Fine, black. I drank too much Calvados. You read three books and mentioned what my father had said on the platform. You asked—in that voice you have—if I could see any soldiers on the beach. I said very funny and told you they had landed farther along the coast. Which made you laugh . . .

Ambrose Zephyr's voice trailed off. A moment later he spasmed himself awake.

Tired, he said, then drifted away again.

When she was certain her husband was well asleep, Zipper walked along the Corniche. She bought a postcard—an amateurish watercolour from some time ago. The bathing tents depicted were green, and judging by the crowds and the queues in the painting, it appeared the beginning of the season.

She returned along the water's edge. The girl in the blue boots had coaxed her dog from the water. Zipper watched them leave, then squinted out to sea.

There was England. Just at the horizon.

E

The Windy Coast of . . . Zipper read, in a tone she reserved for certain circumstances. They were on a train bound for Paris, a flight to Pisa, a short hop to . . .

Elba, said Ambrose.

Just a thought, said Zipper. Why not stay in Paris? Get out of the airport for a while.

Napoleon wasn't keen on the place.

We could take a later flight.

But the views are spectacular.

They will be.

We'll be back to Paris in a few days, Ambrose said. And we always go to Paris. You're not tired of it?

Tired? Yes. Of Paris? No.

How's this then: *E is for Eiffel, a Tower in Paris?*

Zipper pretended to frown. Not quite the music of *The Windy Coast*, she said, but if you don't mind.

Get out of the airport for a while.

Whatever you think.

It was a tone Ambrose could never resist. Nor had ever much tried to.

Zipper awoke in a modest room on the top floor of a hotel—their hotel—tucked in a corner of Place Saint-Sulpice. A band of sunlight found its way between the mismatched towers of the church across the square, through the window and on over the bed. It came to rest across Zipper's face. She slid farther under the duvet, warm and safe.

Home, she thought. Another five minutes. Then

she remembered where she was. Where Ambrose was. Off on his stroll.

——

Whether Ambrose remembered it or not was never the point. The fact remained: they *had* met, and it *was* the first time, on the Rue de Rosiers.

A younger Ambrose Zephyr is midway through his usual walk. Deep in the Marais, a spring downpour forces him into the doorway of an antiquarian bookshop. He huddles, his trench coat dripping on his shoes, and searches the sky for a break. He does not see the young woman coming through the door behind him.

A young Zipper Ashkenazi—on a break from working a fashion shoot—purchases a second-edition *gastronomique* published many years before. The book is in only fair condition and she barters well. A good souvenir, she thinks, of a first trip to Paris. The small volume slips into her coat pocket and she opens the shop door.

Zipper does not see the young man's face as the bell above the door chimes an exit. Ambrose, fretting about his shoes, does not hear the bell.

In the politest French she can manage, Zipper asks the young man's back to excuse her. A startled Ambrose turns and stares at the young woman. Zipper waits, then begins opening her umbrella. Ambrose continues staring, oblivious to weather, shoes, umbrella.

The rain continues.

The staring becomes annoying.

After some time, Zipper breaks the young man's gaze and glances at his feet. Ambrose rediscovers his manners. He steps into the street and allows the woman by. He apologizes in the politest English he can manage. He would have removed his hat, had he owned one.

The rain pours and Ambrose stands watching the young woman disappear under her umbrella. As Zipper steps to avoid a puddle, she glances back at the young man and looks away.

He smiles, having caught her out. She vanishes around a corner and chuckles at the thought of the young Englishman's ruined shoes and drowned hair. A hat, she thinks, might have gone well with the trench and the weather.

Something had changed. The air seemed off. The sunlight through the window felt cold. Zipper thought it might be the cobwebs of a too heavy sleep. She glanced at the bedside clock, padded to the ensuite and ran a bath. By now her husband would be passing Notre-Dame, stepping on the *point zero* marker as he went.

His *flânerie*, Ambrose called it. It was habitual, rarely altered in either route or duration. Friends called it his cliché, mentioning the beaten path, suggesting other sites and different sounds. Ambrose would politely nod his head and wander where he wanted. They have their Paris, he would tell Zipper. I have mine.

She slipped inch by goosebumped inch into the steaming water. Her toes wiggled at the other end of the tub. Zipper closed her eyes as the heat went to her bones, releasing wave after raw wave of terror. She tried imagining something else, but all she could see was their time. Their Paris . . .

The narrow street off the Boulevard Saint-Germain with its family *boulangerie* and two-table cafés and produce stalls. Where they had always bought a workman's lunch and a bottle of *vin de pays*. Where Ambrose would sneak a foul cigarette while she selected a pâté . . .

The Bastille roundabout. Where he would narrow his gaze and point out peasants laying siege to the prison. Where she had mastered the grace of walking in heels amidst the helter-skelter traffic . . .

Zipper's shoulders heaved, she gulped for air, fought for calm. She looked down at her body and thought of his hands.

In Place des Vosges. His hands on her. In the dark beneath Victor Hugo's window, her hands on him.

Breathless mouths, wordless tongues, losing themselves. Under the plane trees in the middle of the night . . .

She buried her face in her hands. *You cannot have it*, she screamed through her fingers.

The antiquarian bookshop. Soon it would belong to other lovers, selfishly claimed as *their* Paris . . .

The *bouquinistes* near the Pont Neuf. He would be there . . .

Zipper pulled herself from the water, hurried to dress, ran for her life.

He would be there by now.

Zipper rushed along the quai towards the Pont Neuf, checked her watch. She was late. Yet she smiled. She knew where he'd be and it wasn't far away and she could slow down.

A *bouquiniste*'s stall caught her eye. It was decorated with the bric-a-brac of the printing trades: agate rulers, bindery clamps, typesetters' trays. A collection of old type blocks.

One particularly worn wooden cube felt soft and good in her hand.

Zipper found Ambrose at the downstream end of Île de la Cité. Lying on the cobbled breakwall that sloped at a comfortable angle into the Seine. He was, as usual, admiring the view along the river to the Eiffel Tower, peeking above the rooftops, far in the distance. Zipper sat beside him.

You smell like cigarettes, she said. How was the walk?

Ambrose lied. Lovely, he said. Zipper caught sight of his slowly trembling hands, the subtle curling and uncurling of fingers.

How was your lie-in? he said. Feel better?

Zipper lied.

As is the habit of lovers in Paris, they spent the rest of the day on the island in the Seine. They ate a workman's lunch, drank all the wine, waved to the *bateau mouche*.

At some point Ambrose lay his head in his wife's lap and stared through the trees to the sky. He said he thought it might rain. Zipper laughed.

Admit it, she said. It *was* you with the soggy shoes. Ambrose smiled.

What remained of the day passed quietly. Without a cloud in sight.

I bought you something, Zipper said. For missing Elba.

They were in a taxi enroute to the airport. She put the wooden type block in his palm and closed his stiff fingers around it. No peeking, she said.

He knew the character by touch. Uppercase, a bold sans serif from a headline tray. He felt the sharp zig and zag of the letterform. The smooth face of the block, the worn and rounded edges. Feels large and heavy for something so small, he said.

I bought you something too. Ambrose handed her a fat and tired edition of *Les Misérables*.

Zipper glanced through the rear window of the

taxi. A tower in Paris, tiny and far away, flashed through the skyline and was gone. The taxi joined the *périphérique*.

F

Late afternoon stretched across the Piazza della Signoria. A marble David—muscular, walleyed, tall for his age—ignored the sightseers crowded about his base. A few with cameras backed away from the horde, cautiously measuring their strides, trying to fit boy king and mugging companions in the viewfinder.

In a quiet corner of a café at the opposite end of the square, Ambrose Zephyr ordered wine. Two glasses. *Rapido*, he snapped.

Zipper was surprised at her husband's tone. She gave him a look he chose to ignore.

They sank low in their chairs. It had not been the day Ambrose had in mind. It had all been too much, too many.

Those who knew Ambrose would later say they were not much surprised by F. After all, they offered, hadn't his mother introduced him—*and at such a young age*—to the great art of Florence? Wasn't he proud—*annoyingly so*—of the university away-term he had spent flirting his way through the city? Did he not know its architects, its Medicis, its masters? By name and date, they said.

An old man moved past their table. He was a picture of the casual Italian gentleman: polished shoes, cufflinks and cravat, practical sunglasses. He carried a walking stick, tapping it lightly on the cobble-stones as he moved along.

The stick missed Ambrose and Zipper's table. There was a minor collision; a drop or two of spilled wine, a stumble. The Italian gentleman apologized as his hand searched for the edge of the table. Ambrose swore under his breath.

Zipper glared at her husband a second time, applying more disgust, less surprise. Ambrose slumped deeper into his chair and sulked at the crowd across the piazza.

No harm done, Zipper said to the Italian gentleman. He turned his body in the direction of her voice and smiled.

Zipper found a third chair. The old gentleman asked if he might rest. Just for a moment . . . the joints, you see.

You smell like my wife, he said. Zipper was embarrassed by her suddenly blushed cheeks.

When we would walk. In our evenings along the river, she wore that fragrance. A wise and clever woman, my wife. This I know, she would say: A man can see a hundred women, lust for a thousand more, but it is one scent that will open his eyes and turn him to love. And he will never thank the angels for making him blow his nose that morning.

The sightseers under the marble boy king grew more boisterous.

These crowds, said the Italian gentleman. They take many photographs. Such a sad thing. Such a long way to come to take bad pictures of one's friends.

He shrugged. This city is too much for them. he said. Too many paintings, too many churches, too many Davids. Too many other people taking pictures. Can you see the Duomo? someone will ask. I can see the back of your head, another will answer.

But enough, he blurted in Ambrose's direction. Life is too quick for such gloom. There are other things to see.

Ambrose scowled.

The old gentleman searched for Zipper's hand. Indulge me a bit of a game, he said. He took her hand and cupped it between his.

Signora's blouse, he announced after a moment, is as white as our marble. Crisp and tailored, like a man's. The cuffs are rolled, the collar is turned. Very casual. The buttons open just so and—forgive me, signora—there is perhaps a peek of black lace, a peek of something.

A smile inched across Ambrose's face. The gentleman continued.

She wears a silk scarf—reds and golds, I think. A flowing skirt, calf length. Red again, like Il Papa's cardinals. But it is late in the day—she has slid her sunglasses to the top of her head. A strand of hair hangs to the side of her face. She squints with the low sun. The feet of birds at the corners of her eyes. Have I missed anything?

Signora's shoes, offered Ambrose.

Aaaah, said the Italian gentleman, there you are. Now you wish to play my game. Very well.

They are . . . black. Yes. Flat. For too much rushing around. For too many people. For too much art. But I am guessing. Better, I think, for walking by the river?

Ambrose looked at his wife. Zipper noticed it was the first time his eyes had brightened all day.

A third glass was summoned and a toast to marble kings was drunk. Ambrose apologized for his behaviour. Not my best day, he said. The Italian gentleman said there was no harm done. Ambrose asked him about his wife.

The old gentleman produced a small photograph and handed it to Ambrose. I have many, he said. They never seem to be where I leave them.

Ambrose smiled. He passed the photograph to Zipper.

She expected an old and faded portrait of a young and beautiful woman. Instead, the face that smiled stiffly from the photo was worn, fleshy, a little pale. But the eyes were clear, the hair well styled. An expensive scarf was tied loosely around the old woman's neck.

The face in the photograph had been embossed. Raised creases and furrows traced the features: scarf, hair, eyes. The shy smile.

I think she might be like your own signora, the Italian gentleman said. Something to see?

She was, said Ambrose. Is.

The Italian gentleman finished his wine and stood as best he could. He kissed Zipper's hand, begging forgiveness for leaving so abruptly.

I promised to meet someone by the river, he said, and tapped his walking stick across the piazza. As he passed the marble boy king, he pulled his pocket square with a flourish and quietly blew his nose.

The Mediterranean was passing far below them, Zipper Ashkenazi nudged her husband. You were talking, she said.

Sorry . . . dozed off . . . what? What did I say?

You kept asking why.

Why what?

I don't know. You were asleep.

Must have been dreaming.

Of?

A woman in the distance, approaching. She wades carefree through the desert sand. She looks back towards the sun. She is barefoot, her sandals clutched by the heels, dangling in one hand. Her other hand holds the hem of her white cotton robe. Each step trails a fine stream of sand, caught in the hot wind and blown towards the Nile. The sun backlights her figure through the cotton, catches a glint of silver and ebony on her bracelets. Her walk in the desert has left her flushed and bronzed. Her hair is dark and fine.

A camel appears from nowhere, blocking the view. Everything swirls into the art on a package of cigarettes.

A boy lies on his bedroom floor. He is twelve, perhaps thirteen years old. He is drawing, with painstaking accuracy, the art from a pack of Camels. The arabesque curves of the serifs on the A. The ellipsed E. Three palm trees, two pyramids, one camel with its skinny legs. The pyramids tucked under the camel's sagging belly. The boy is careful, colouring the camel's visible eye a brilliant blue. He even includes the elegant ampersand between the words *Turkish* and *Domestic*.

The camel turns his head and grins.

Why so sad, Master Zephyr?

The boy frowns.

Death? Yes yes, death hovers near us all. And it is sad that it makes us sad. But I know a story.

There once was a camel whose days begin in the shade of a palm on a nameless wadi, somewhere to the east of here. In the Sinai.

By the age of ten, the camel is a veteran of the trading routes from Alexandria to Tripoli. At twenty he walks the rich Aswan run, kneeling politely as nervous Japanese women climb aboard to have their portraits taken. At thirty he is done working, his knees worn thin. At forty, his days as a camel come to a peaceful end. Eyeing younger things in the Birqash market.

He is gutted and skinned. For seven days he

feeds his owner, his owner's family, his owner's cousins, his owner's neighbours. His hide is sold for a good and fair price in the bazaar, to a maker of furniture who knows a good many buttocks would sit on such a fine and worthy leather.

Was there anything before his days as a camel, you ask? Yes yes, Master Zephyr. The camel was a man. As you will be. Successful, well fed, loved by a clever and honest and beautiful woman. Happy they lived. Simply as husband and wife. Without extravagance, just off the high road between Suez and Aqaba.

The man misses his wife every day. Even now, as a camel in your drawing, as a comfortable chair under a large rump. But he sees her every day. He watches her sleep.

Why, you ask? There is no why, Master Zephyr. It is just a story. Life goes on. Death goes on. Love goes on. It is all as simple as that. Years from now, even you will return. Perhaps as the ochre that colours an artist's brush. Or a kindly stray cat in a small park in London. And you will love the birds you chase.

And then the camel winked, said Ambrose, and disappeared in a puff of sand.

Zipper blinked away a tear. He hadn't meant to make her cry.

G

The small bedouin woman sat on her haunches beneath the pyramids.

Her robes were black and billowed in the wind. She smoked a dark cigarette and played with a small Polaroid camera: holding it to the sunshine, tracing circles in front of her face, mimicking a self-photograph, watching for the soft image to emerge from its slot. She cooed and chirped and sang to herself. As a child might. Her grinning revealed the gaps of a few missing teeth.

She kept her place, apart from the mob of touts

with their curative river water and stuffed crocodiles and plastic scarabs. Tourists scurried and counted out their dollars and pounds and yen and avoided her altogether.

Zipper noticed the woman, as Ambrose was otherwise occupied. He stood to the shade side of the cornerstone and leaned in to sight the edge of the Great Pyramid of Khufu. He closed his eyes to slits, gauging the angle of the corner, the smoothness of finishing stones, the tiny army of labourers far above. Naked and sweating and laying the final course.

Zipper left her husband and jostled away from the crowds. She found a quiet spot and sat in the hot sand. She watched the bedouin woman. Zipper wondered who or what was in the woman's photographs.

The woman stopped her play, beckoned Zipper. Come come, she said. Sit sit. There is nothing to be afraid of.

Ambrose leaned his face against the stone. He ran his hands across the rough surface, following a groove here, fingering a worn edge, clearing the grit from a notch there. Checking for true.

Hush hush, said the woman.

Your singing is beautiful, Zipper said.

And you are afraid.

Zipper's heart thumped in her ears. She felt her hands go cold.

I should get back, she said. My husband . . .

I know what you see, the old woman said. What frightens you. But what you see you must not fear.

Zipper's eyes welled up.

Everything will be well, the woman said. For you. For your husband.

Zipper wiped her face and forced a smile.

The sign admonished visitors: To Climb Or Scale Or Deface The Sacred Tombs Is Highly Forbidden In Order To Protect Their Fragile And Historical Nature.

Ambrose Zephyr likely thought otherwise. Nothing so enormous and so immortal could be that precarious.

Or that tempting.

—

Yes yes. Hold his hand. He will not be away so long. Not so long.

As she spoke, the bedouin woman turned to watch a man struggling to climb the pyramid.

Zipper followed the woman's gaze to find her husband standing on the cornerstone of the first course of the Great Pyramid. Ambrose was hunched over, hands braced on his knees, wheezing and coughing.

The photograph is amateurish: the horizon tilting wildly, the subjects fuzzy and almost out of frame, a blurred black fingertip across one corner. In the photograph a man stands atop a great stone block, stiff and uncomfortable, beaming and posing as best he can. Like a schoolboy Lawrence, awkward but having gotten away with something.

He is pale in the dusky sun. His linen suit is scuffed and wrinkled and has become too large. Below him, a woman stands shy and reluctant. She is flushed, gently tanned, but appears lost.

H

Somewhere between the Giza plateau and Cairo their taxi ran out of petrol. The subsequent bus rattled and inched along with the city's traffic. There were no seats and no handholds. There was something that sounded like no brakes.

When Ambrose Zephyr and his wife arrived at the airport, a sudden sandstorm had closed the runways, briefly but effectively.

Connections, and Haifa, were missed.

I

It would have been clear to those queuing for the flight, had they noticed, that the Englishman was having difficulty.

Ambrose Zephyr's face was drained white. He smelt foul, soiled, rotten in his own sweat. He stretched and curled and twisted his hands, rubbed his joints, cringed when he stood, shivered in the airport heat. Every few minutes his eyes bulged in their dark sockets. Like those of a person afraid of something he could hear or smell but not see.

He snapped at his wife after she had asked

him, again, if there was anything she could do.

I am fine, Ambrose croaked.

Is there anything you need? Zipper forced the question through her teeth.

I need to be left alone.

Zipper wanted to throw something at him.

Enough, he said.

Hit him.

Stop fussing, he said.

Stop him. Stop it. Go home.

Ambrose seemed to recover as the queue moved to board the flight to Istanbul.

They sat in the last row: Ambrose, Zipper and an enormous young man who said that he was flying to visit his sister she is a nice dancer in a hotel viewing the Bosporus saving money for hospitality school so she may return to our family's taverna back home nice to meet you English couple on holiday I am presuming I study my English very much and you should come to our taverna someday such a nice

couple you are though sir you do not look so well
perhaps it is the flying maybe do you smell something? Where was I yes my sister the belly dancer
she will help me and our father who is being most
lonely since our mother left to be with her sister
who is my aunt and raises many goats and makes
their cheese best in all the Mediterranean yes now
the card yes here it is the hotel where there is a view
and my sister dances come if you are feeling well
perhaps a *hamam* could help sir yes Turkish bath very
good for all ailments can bring the dead back to life
for madame as well I very highly recommend but
remember please the hotel where my sister dances
and sees the Bosporus if you get a chance my sister
really is most good at the dancing perhaps a little
heavy in the hips she should lose some weight but
then who shouldn't ha ha there I think we are here
and landed you nice English couple have a nice day
it is a pleasure to be flying with you now remember
you come and visit my family's taverna someday best
coffee in all the Mediterranean truly even better than

Istanbul perhaps we will see each other again remember a Turkish bath will do you no harm try the bath near the Blue Mosque very old very safe I know it well sorry let me slide over a little so you can get by apologies yes it is small in here I am perhaps too big for such a little airplane ha ha here let me move my so sorry can you get your leg over there okay sorry just a bit further maybe if I inhale a bit.

Walking to the taxi rank, Ambrose told Zipper that he had once imagined a view across the Bosporus. Or had seen it in a movie. He couldn't recall which.

Perhaps, said Zipper, a proper Turkish bath will clear your head. At the least the smell.

As boys of thirteen or fourteen are prone to do, Ambrose Zephyr received his first lesson regarding the intrigues of the near East, and sex, from a woman.

The woman in question was not Polly or Penny

or Patsy what-was-her-name who had lived a few doors down. Prunella or Poppy or Priscilla was the gangly one. Breastless, with braces that cut his lip during a stolen kiss in his parents' garden.

No. The woman in question worked for the wrong side but longed to work for the right side. She was willing and well able to use her nakedness under clinging bedsheets. She was born on the steppes of Russia, nimble with a code machine and a gun, breasted, blond, and in possession of a suite overlooking the Bosporus.

Her name was Tatiana, said Ambrose as he and Zipper got out of the taxi in front of the oldest bathhouse in the city.

Of course it was, said Zipper.

And Bond meets her in the hotel room, said Ambrose.

The one with the view?

Right. She's wearing nothing but a silk ribbon around her neck. Completely naked, and our man in a dinner jacket. Imagine that.

Imagine that.

Zipper thought of a polite and curious boy of thirteen or fourteen years, sitting alone in a cinema. Possibly a matinee near Piccadilly Circus. His eyes bugging at the views of Istanbul.

Zipper emerged from the women's side of the baths to find her husband attempting to brush the wrinkles and smell from his suit. His hair was slicked flat to his head, his face was flushed and shaved, his smile was broad. A child freshly plucked from the Sunday tub. Zipper's expression was black, her face drained of everything but anger.

How was your bath? Ambrose asked.

Excruciating, said Zipper.

Large attendant?

Amazonian.

Small towel?

Humiliating.

Steam?

I've had enough.

Luffah glove?

You need to deal with this.

Massage?

That is not it.

Oil? Liniments? Palm fronds?

THAT IS NOT THE POINT.

Zipper stared at her husband in disbelief. They were still standing in front of the Velázquez Venus.

I mean yes, that is a point. Just not the point.

Sorry, said Ambrose.

Stop apologizing.

Sorry.

The point is you never say anything. I haven't a clue what you think about anything important.

Sorry.

Stop it. Stop being so damned . . . absent.

Ambrose shrugged.

Don't you care about anything? I mean really have an opinion. Beyond *it's lovely*?

Fine, said Ambrose. If you must know. I think the

Velázquez is remarkable because it doesn't matter to me that she was an actress or that the sheets are black. I think abstract expressionism is crap. I think Brussels sprouts are crap. I think I could paint but I don't have the nerve. I think I am an unbelievably lucky man who is married to a woman who I think looks a little like the Rokeby Venus and I think if I open my mouth to say something I think is important I think she will discover she's married a fool.

You are many things my love. A fool is not one of them. You're imagining things.

I am keeping things to myself. Having an opinion doesn't require sharing it with everybody.

It requires sharing it with me. Because *I* get to know what you think. *I* get to know you better than anyone else.

You do. Always have, always will, full stop. Let it go.

One more thing.

What?

You're wrong.

Am I?

Luck had nothing to do with us.

Outside the baths, Ambrose's scrubbed smile disappeared. THEN WHAT IS THE POINT?, he said, smoothing another crease in his suit. Deal with what? What would you have me do?

Care. Worry. Say something. Aren't you afraid?

Yes.

So?

So what? So there it is. Here I am. There's nothing to deal with. If there were I would do it. But there isn't and I am terrified and this isn't happening to you.

You selfish, silent, shitty bastard. This *is* happening to me.

Really? In less than a month, you'll still be alive.

Really. I can hardly wait. Lying in on Sundays? At last. A decent cup of tea? Brilliant. No more squinting, no more visions, no more imagination, no more silence? I can hardly fucking wait.

—

In a lane near the Blue Mosque, around the corner from the oldest bathhouse in the city, curious pedestrians might have noticed a rumpled Englishman embracing a sobbing woman as if she might fly apart. She struggled to free herself, he held tighter. He whispered, she lashed out. He kissed her wet eyes, she turned her face away.

After a moment or two, the woman said she was fine. The Englishman handed her a thin bauble, a *boncuk*. He told her that Turkish mothers pin the blue glass trinket to their children's clothes. To keep them safe.

The curious might have watched for a few more moments and then moved along and thought nothing more of it.

That evening Ambrose and Zipper found a bench in a corner of the gardens of Topkapi Palace, where grand and terrible sultans had once lived. Ambrose claimed the sultans had attended to the needs of their harems in this garden. After they had emerged from their baths, he said. Zipper said that sounded like something only a man would think up.

In the sultan's garden, Zipper and Ambrose stole as much love as they dared. A few buttons undone. Straps moved gently aside. The slip of a warm hand. The smell of bath oil and perfumed soap. Luffahed skin, sensitive to the touch. They whispered to each other not to worry.

The evening deepened and the lights on the Asian side grew more numerous. Zipper asked where the *boncuk* had come from. Ambrose said he had bought it while waiting for his lover to emerge from her bath.

They sat for a while longer and wondered whether the nice hotel dancer would ever get back to the taverna and whether she was as good as her brother had advertised.

In my opinion, said Ambrose, the best in all the Mediterranean.

The next morning near sunrise, London called nine times in as many minutes. None were answered.

Four calls came from Zipper's office, two from the offices of D&C. No messages left. One call just kept yelling *pick up, pick up, pick up, pick up*. One was from the Foreign Office: *In town. Drinks?* The ninth call left a message: *Sir's shirts are ready and may be picked up at his leisure as it were.*

Ambrose stood at the hotel window, looking at the Bosporus through the dawn haze. He wavered slightly, leaning his forehead against the pane to catch his balance. It was time to go home, Zipper announced, knowing her husband would never admit so on his own.

Ambrose turned and managed a sad smile. Home then?

Home then.

They slept that night in their own bed in the narrow Victorian terrace in Kensington.

J, and the shirts, could wait.

K

Ambrose Zephyr stood shaving in his bathroom.

His wife hovered in the doorway, watching her husband's hands. A subtle tremor, more noticeable in the right. The razor hand. Ambrose leaned into the fogged mirror and pulled a slow stroke. His hands steadied. The knot in Zipper's stomach eased.

We can't keep avoiding them, Zipper said as her husband finished his neck and began on his chin.

I'd rather not be today's topic, said Ambrose.

Friends wouldn't do that.

Zipper stood beside her husband and rested her

head against his shoulder. Ambrose looked at her reflection in the mirror. What he could make out appeared hollow. As if she wasn't quite there.

Everyone does it, said Ambrose. One minute you are who you are. The next it's strange looks and wringing hands and poor Ambrose is there anything we can do Ambrose let's all dance on eggshells Ambrose. Suddenly it's all that you are. All you will be.

Ambrose held out his razor hand and watched the tremor shake a few drops of water to the floor. This, he said, is not me.

He looked back at the mirror. They, he said, are not us.

When the Mankowitzes lived at twenty-six and the Ashkenazis lived at thirty, the girls would meet in front of twenty-eight. Neighbours said that *with that pair*, that Katerina Mankowitz and Zappora Ashkenazi, there was always much to decide. What to do about boys. What to do about Katerina's beastly little sister. What to do about their hair, their shoes, their skin. Zappora called her best friend Kitts.

When Kitts found a job as a photographer's assistant, she put a word in with her employer regarding a friend looking for work.

When Kitts thought she was pregnant, Zappora found a discreet clinic. As it turned out Kitts was late. The friends celebrated at the local. Zappora bought a round for the house.

When Zipper announced she had met someone, Kitts approved. As long as he can be trusted, she said. It was Kitts who found the wedding dress.

When Kitts left her most recent lover, Zipper made up the spare room. She used some of Kitts's photography to decorate. Kitts would never say as much, but what hung on the walls was worth thousands. Moody black-and-whites of backlane characters in rough countries were much in demand by the world's collectors.

Pick up, pick up, pick up, pick up. PICK UP.

Zipper answered the phone.

Kitts said she was on her way.

Ambrose opened his front door and found Kitts glowering at him. She was, as always, tall and haggard. Like a woman just returned from working in a place with no running water. She called Ambrose a bastard and hugged him. Longer and warmer than usual.

Lovely to see you too, said Ambrose as Kitts went inside. He sat on his front step and lit a cigarette left over from Paris.

In her kitchen, through two pots of tea, Zipper came apart. She started laughing like a schoolgirl. L is for List, she said. W is for Was It Something I Did? D is for Something I Didn't Do? S is for Something I Should Have Done?

She showed Kitts the journal, fanning the pages like a conjuror. She pulled odd items from the journal's envelope. Souvenirs, Zipper said. What a grand bloody tour it's been.

Other bits and baubles materialized from Zipper's pockets. Everything formed a small mound on the table.

A postcard featuring a muddy reproduction of an enormous Rembrandt.

A is for a Portrait in Amsterdam, said Zipper.

A small and smooth stone, grey and warm.

Barbaric Berlin.

A flattened lavender bloom, barely fragrant.

Advertising in Chartres.

Another postcard, this time offering a jolly water-coloured *Bienvenue à Deauville*.

A honeymoon by the sea, Zipper said.

A fat and worn copy of *Les Misérables*, an embossed photograph of an Italian woman in an elegant scarf, an unflattering Polaroid snap of Ambrose and Zipper by the Pyramids. A child's blue glass bauble.

Our Paris, laughed Zipper. Florence, Giza, Istanbul. Did I mention we missed Haifa?

Zipper picked up the journal. Page after blank page.

And what will I have when he's gone? Nothing. No growing ancient together, no retiring to the *pied-à-terre*, no children, no grandchildren come to that. No more. No life. Nothing. Blank.

But you never wanted children, Kitts said.

I never wanted this. I is for I Don't Know What to Do.

Kitts sat in the eye of her friend's storm, nodded, shook her head, held tight, wiped Zipper's dripping face, put the kettle on, wept, buttressed, agreed. Listened.

When the worst had passed, Kitts did what she had done since the childhood meetings in front of twenty-eight. She said something smart at the precise moment when there was nothing to say.

He's right, the bastard. Live what's left. Live it as large as you both can. That's what he wants. *That's* what you want.

Zipper threw her journal on the table.

But the words. How do I start? Where do I end?

The words will come, said Kitts. They always do.

Wilkes and Zephyr met at university.

They took a loose interest in the other's academics: Ambrose sneaking his friend into a life-drawing class to prove that artists did not get erections; Freddie instructing his friend on the proper balance between single malts and thesis writing.

After graduating, they shared a shoebox flat in a hard part of London and lied on each other's cv. They began referring to each other by last name only. It sounded good, they'd explain. Something professionals might do.

When it appeared likely they were destined to drive cabs, Wilkes passed his foreign service examinations and Zephyr landed a junior position as a copywriter. Which, much later in their lives, they would characterize as ironic.

Between distant postings and demanding clientele, the friends rarely saw each other. They never reminisced when they did. They kept every piece of wish-you-were-here correspondence and look-what-I-created souvenir each had sent the other.

No one, least of all Zipper, could explain why they had remained friends for so long and at such distance. Or why they had even become friends in the first place.

Drinks? always meant the Savoy bar.

All Ambrose would later say about his evening with Freddie was how good it had been to see an old friend. They spent the time talking mostly of each other's work, said Ambrose. State secrets, slagged clients, that sort of thing.

What likely occurred was that after enough kirs and enough whiskeys, Ambrose reluctantly described the circumstances. There would have been long silences, pinched glances, calls for same again please.

After some time the friends would have found their Gallipoli courage and looked each other in the face. There would have been tears in their eyes. Stoic ones, but tears nonetheless.

Damn, Freddie likely said, turning away for a moment.

Ambrose probably apologized.

The friends would have pulled themselves together. Freddie, as always, would then have said something clever and wise.

You need to edit. Enough with A through Zed. Toss the list. You'll end up hating half the places you go anyway. Think of Zipper. Stop dragging the woman about. Wasn't she the one who said it was time to come home?

At the end of the evening, the friends would have stood on the street waiting for taxis. They would have embraced, as old friends do when parting. If you need anything, Freddie no doubt said.

Right then.

Right.

Taxis would have appeared.

Neither friend would have said goodbye. They never had before.

J

Ambrose Zephyr would sometimes remark that a better man was one supplied with an intelligent woman, the ability to tango and an able tailor.

For those who knew Ambrose, *an able tailor* became the explanation for why Ambrose Zephyr had stroked out Jaipur on his list and pencilled in Old Jewry.

Mr Umtata sailed from home a younger man, stowed away in the hold of a runt freighter. When the authorities realized he was gone, he wasn't missed.

Good riddance, they said. Another kaffir away.

On the day the freighter docked in London, Germany was invading its neighbours. A week later Mr Umtata found work in the army. Nothing at the sharp end of course, they said. You understand. Still doing your bit as it were.

He learned a trade. Mind the break at the cuff, Major would say. A bit snug across the shoulder. Give those buttons a polish, there's a good fellow. Mr Umtata's war raged through the officers' mess. When it ended Major and his buttons went home to the country and Mr Umtata went to Cheapside.

He took up piecework in a ladies and gents shop. Alterations To All Garments Our Specialty The Smartest Styles Within Bespoke Orders Upon Request Satisfaction Assured For All Closed Sundays. He enjoyed the ladies' work particularly.

He learned how to dance. To understand how the clothes move, he told his employer. Mr Umtata was a small man whose teeth were too big for his mouth, but his partners did not mind. He was always impeccably dressed, he smelled heavenly and he could move. Like Astaire himself, they said.

After twenty years Mr Umtata purchased the shop. It was a narrow concern, too dark in summer, too hot in winter, and could neither boast nor hold the selection common among the Savile shops. But Mr Umtata's handwork was slow and sure, his service humble, his discretion reliable. Observation and counsel were parcelled out as he saw fit. Upon request.

They met the morning a younger Ambrose Zephyr produced his first television commercial: thirty seconds for the finest cleanser the mod '70s housewife could ever wish to own.

The concept involved a red-haired actress, grinning in a mod '70s housewife manner, on her knees scrubbing the average English street—a tip to the product's mod '70s scouring power. What the woman's hot pants tipped to was left to interpretation. Old Jewry stood in as average street.

The commercial was to be filmed from an extreme

angle and Ambrose had split the seat out of his trousers checking the first setup of the day. An assistant from the agency shoved him through Umtata's door for repairs. The tailor's first advice: a proper fit through the buttocks.

When asked by Ambrose what he thought of the activity in the street, Mr Umtata replied that it all appeared interesting but sir may want to reconsider the hot pants.

Ambrose became as regular a customer as wages and wear would allow. Jackets now and then, shirts by the gross, flirtations with bellbottomed trousers (against contrary advice). At the rear of the shop, in a wooden box marked Active, Mr Umtata kept a file card with particulars: *Zephyr, A. Dresses left, favours right shoulder, prefers contrasting linings. Poor colour sense. Requires some direction. See also Ashkenazi, Z (Mrs)*. It was the only card filed under Z.

Ambrose brought Zipper to Old Jewry to meet Mr Umtata, as a young suitor intent on impressing might. Do you approve? asked Ambrose.

Indeed sir, said Mr Umtata. I believe the expression is yin to your yang. And if I may be so bold sir. Does the lady dance?

Mr Umtata cut, lined and hand-stitched the suit Ambrose was married in—double breasted, trousers in the full and classic style, startling yellow tie. At his final fitting, with Zipper observing, Ambrose suggested a matching yellow carnation for the lapel. Zipper rolled her eyes. Mr Umtata frowned in silence.

I think it makes a statement, don't you? said Ambrose.

Indeed sir, said Mr Umtata.

Just the thing for the big day.

Quite.

Bit much?

As you say sir.

Mr Umtata also fit and altered Zipper's dress (an off-white vintage number, one previous owner, purchased in Portobello Road). With my compliments missus, Mr Umtata said as he snipped the last thread and stood aside to allow Zipper a full look in the mirror.

The lady does indeed dance, said Zipper as she swished.

Mr Umtata and Zipper then toasted her impending marriage with a deep and expert dip. To ensure proper movement, said Mr Umtata through a toothy smile.

On the day, the newlyweds looked like famous people, despite the downpour in Kensington Gardens. Zipper's bouquet was a handful of small white rosebuds. Complemented by a small white rosebud in Ambrose's lapel. Mr Umtata was unable to attend. Saturday was a brisk day at the shop in Old Jewry. He sent regrets.

Years later the wedding suit still fit. The linen number, however, was in urgent need of attention. And there was the matter of shirts being ready.

At the rear of the shop, Mr Umtata uttered a stream of sighs. Ambrose asked if anything could be done.

Zipper mentioned time was pressing. Mr Umtata then suggested sir might strip to his boxers. Missus might want to take a seat.

In silence the tailor of Old Jewry worked his needles and threads and scissors and irons. Ambrose searched for somewhere to put his hands. Zipper watched her husband's white skin, stretched thin over bone.

We've been abroad, said Ambrose.

Indeed sir, said Mr Umtata through the pins between his teeth.

Rather suddenly.

Indeed.

Travelled light.

So it would seem sir.

Sorry for the rush.

As am I sir, said Mr Umtata, hiding the last seam, his eyes fixed on Zipper's wet eyes.

A fresh shirt was unwrapped. Ambrose strained out a smile as he dressed.

A miracle, Umtata. As always.

As you say sir.

A bit loose across the shoulders though.

Indeed sir. Shall we check the fit?

With that Mr Umtata took Ambrose Zephyr in his arms. Allow me the lead sir, he whispered. The men dipped. Deeply, expertly.

Zipper Ashkenazi laughed out loud. For the first time in days.

L

The sun began to rise as Ambrose Zephyr sat on his front step. It was, still, his best time of the day.

He watched number twelve with his tiny dog. The elderly man frowned: he had forgotten his hat. Number eighteen, naked this morning and trusting that no one was awake at such an hour, gathered the morning paper from her doorstep. The neighbourhood stray, ignored, eyed the birds in the park across the way.

The night fog burned off. For Zipper Ashkenazi, standing at her front window wearing one of her husband's new shirts, it looked to be a rare morning. A fine one, for the time of year.

Ambrose sipped his coffee, certain his wife was catching just five minutes more. He waved to number eighteen and sheepishly smiled an apology for having seen more than he should have. The elderly man went home to get his hat.

Zipper waited until the sun came through the front window, then made a cup of tea. She joined her husband on the front step.

I need to deal with the office, Ambrose said.

Zipper watched the neighbourhood stray.

Loose ends, that sort of thing.

Zipper examined the dregs in her cup.

I should have called, she said.

Near Leicester Square stood the offices of Dravot, Carnehan. A few streets away stood the offices of the third most-read fashion magazine in the country. Zipper and Ambrose had managed to work in the same part of the city, but neither one could remember when they had managed lunch together. Or ridden the underground as a couple off to work. Isn't it funny, thought Zipper, to be doing that now. They decided D&C would be first and best dealt with.

Few heads turned as Ambrose and Zipper walked through the creative department to his office. Everyone is too fresh, thought Zipper. Too busy. Too young.

Greta sat in Ambrose's chair, looking out the windows and fidgeting with his collection of type blocks. Without turning around she said how odd it all felt. D&C had gotten the account.

I'll just clear up a few things, said Ambrose.

More annoying than odd, actually, said Greta.

I won't be long.

Big meeting next week. Strategy.

Most of it you can toss.

Tactics. New staff.

The plants are fake. They'll last.

Global campaign. Much work to do.

Just a few things.

The billing will be huge . . .

Greta's voice trailed out through the window.

Ambrose picked over his desk. A photograph of himself at a location shoot: longer hair, horrid bell-bottomed trousers, a red-haired actress nearby. A newspaper style manual. A pocket atlas, leather-bound with ribbon marker. A few travel brochures from the '60s: *Ski Zermatt This Year, Beautiful St. Moritz, Now Is the Time for Geneva*. A moody black-and-white photograph of Zipper. Taken in a rough country in a younger time.

You can keep the type, said Ambrose. My gift.

Greta turned away from the window. Tears flowed down her cheeks and dripped from her chin.

Bloody annoying, she said.

Yes it is, said Ambrose.

I hate this. I want to go home.

I hear Berlin is lovely this time of year.

Ambrose smiled and kissed Greta warmly on both cheeks. He pocketed the photograph of Zipper and left.

Pru was yelling at Milan or Paris or New York or her assistant when Zipper appeared at her door. Pru threw her earpiece across the room, glanced at Ambrose as if he wasn't there and began yelling at Zipper.

I quit, said Zipper. Her life had unravelled. It didn't need Pru picking at the threads. She wished *quit* had come out sounding angrier.

YOU WILL NEVER write again, Pru said as quietly as her disposition could manage. I WILL SEE TO IT.

Perhaps you will, said Zipper.

MNOPQRSTU

It took most of the day for Ambrose and Zipper to reach Hyde Park. Here and there Ambrose's gait had slowed to the shuffle of an old man. Crowded pavements and clogged traffic had taken their own toll.

Through Kensington Gardens the pace improved. In other times, on better strolls, Ambrose would say he could see the King out for his morning ride: mounted on a dapple grey, overdressed in lace and buckles, the court blundering behind him like a bad comedy sketch.

They stopped to rest at the edge of the Round Pond. Canvas deckchairs had been put out for the season. Ambrose looked across the water and the swans and into nothing.

What would you have done, Zipper asked.

I would have sat on a beach in Mumbai, said Ambrose, and had my hair cut. For extra rupees the barber would have told my fortune. *Sahib will be leading a surprising life.* You would have worn a sari the colour of aubergine.

New York. I'd been there once. On business? No. You were there. For the spring shows. Did you take me along? Or was it business? Funny how I can't recall. It was much farther away than I remembered.

O. O . . . is Osaka. I bow to the department store hostesses, they cover their smiles when they hear my Japanese. You and I are at the theatre. *Bunraku* I think they call it here. A tragic tale. Montagues and Capulets, judging by the acting. You cry during the final act. P. Pago Pago. Paddington. Perth? I learn a new language, Queensland gone walkabout. We waltzed, didn't we? The beach . . .

—

There was an odd half-smile on Ambrose's face. He looked away.

Keep going, said Zipper. Please keep going.

What?

R. You were about to say R.

. . . Rio . . . the beach. Ipanema. They have professional foot washers imagine that I can see Africa from the beach and you are not so young or tall but very tanned and quite lovely and there's Shanghai sea of tai chi women scowling at me a tiny string ensemble of five-year-olds playing something in a minor Barber's *Adagio* sad for such little hands . . .

Don't stop, said Zipper.

I can't.

T?

Can't remember. Timbuktu?

Don't worry. U then.

Ambrose looked at his wife as if he didn't know her. The King, he said, is not much of a horseman.

Oh God.

Ambrose and Zipper did not move until dark. The panic was slow to ease.

The moon rose above the treetops and they walked the rest of the way home. As they turned into their road, Ambrose said he remembered.

V

We were staying in a *pensione* near the Piazza San Marco. I woke up too early. It was difficult putting on the linen number in the dark, but I didn't want to wake you. I borrowed a blanket from the hotel and walked across the piazza.

Everything was mist and fog. It was raining, softly, off and on. The air felt cold for the time of year. It was too early for the cafés to open.

I found a chair and pulled it to a better spot near the lagoon. The gondolas were still tied to their posts, bobbing like toy boats. I wrapped myself in the blanket and soaked in the hazy view across the lagoon. In all the years we talked about Venice and pictured Venice and dreamed of Venice, did we ever once imagine it might smell?

I was sleeping when you found me. You said you had worried. I'm fine, I said. How could I not be? I've kept a promise.

You smiled and said yes, finally, I had.

The waiters were unstacking chairs, wiping tables, opening umbrellas. The piazza began filling with tourists bundled against the chill, griping about the weather, trying to fit the Campanile in the viewfinder.

You and I left the edge of the lagoon and went off in search of breakfast. We found the Bridge of Sighs, lost our way to the Erberia, and decided we weren't hungry anyway. We were wet and cold and our clothes reeked of dead fish and it couldn't have mattered less.

Zipper said that was how she remembered it as well.

Z

I'll be along in a minute, Ambrose said. Zipper went upstairs and crawled on top of the duvet. She stared at the ceiling.

What felt like hours later Ambrose appeared at the bedroom door. Zipper helped him into bed, wrapped him in an extra blanket to stop the shivering, curled herself around him. She was drifting in and out of sleep when the air in the Victorian terrace turned suddenly thick. The silence startled her awake.

Zipper cried quietly for a long while before ringing Kitts and Freddie. They would know what to do, whom to call.

She kissed her husband's eyes and went downstairs.

On the kitchen table she found her well-thumbed edition of *Wuthering Heights*, a ragged slip of paper tucked in the first few pages. *Chapter One. 1801—I have just returned from a visit . . .*

On the paper, Zanzibar had been scribbled over. In the margin was written *Zipper.* With the proper amount of swoosh to the Z, and in a remarkably steady hand.

A few evenings later, Zipper Ashkenazi sat on her doorstep under a threatening sky. She wore a borrowed linen jacket, too large across the shoulders, but warm enough against a stiff spring breeze. Beside her stood the leather suitcase from under the bed.

She watched number twelve carry his tiny dog around the park. Number eighteen hurried along the pavement, a few minutes behind her time. The neighbourhood stray strolled towards the birds.

When the elderly man passed by, he paused. He

put down the dog and turning smartly towards Zipper, took off his hat and bowed. The dog stood unsettled at his master's feet, trying to ignore the neighbourhood stray. The man replaced his hat, collected his dog and walked slowly home.

Number eighteen kept walking past her waiting children and stopped a step or two below Zipper. The woman's smile was shy. After a moment she found something to say. She told Zipper that she had always enjoyed her column in the fashion magazine. It was the first thing she read every month. You always have an interesting story to tell, she said.

There was another pause. Yes, well, the woman said finally. Tea, she suggested, might be nice. Perhaps . . . sometime . . . when you're ready then.

Zipper thanked the woman for her kindness. Tea would be brilliant. Soon. The woman's children waved their art, and off she went.

Zipper sat for a while longer, watching the empty park. It began to rain. She opened the journal that had come from the bookshop in Amsterdam. With slow and gentle care, Zipper emptied the contents of the envelope into Ambrose's suitcase. From a pocket of her jacket she pulled a type block. Boldface, sans serif. She paused, then put the worn wooden cube back where it belonged.

She turned to the journal's first page, wiped her hand down its blank face, thought for a moment, and began to write.

This story is unlikely.

ACKNOWLEDGEMENTS

For friendship and editorial wisdom nonpareil: Laura Barber, Martha Kanya-Forstner.

For representation in the face of all reason: Suzanne Brandreth, Dean Cooke. In London: Will Francis, Antony Topping.

At Portobello, the good hands of Philip Gwyn Jones, Hannah Marshall, Tasja Dorkofikis, Sally Wilson. And beyond: Andy Bridge, Patty Rennie, Daniel Scott.

For patience, enthusiasm, and Ambrose's suitcase: Hannah Richardson, Sanger Richardson.

And for saying yes: Rebecca Richardson, without whom the above would have never read a word, nor applied their characteristic expertise, grace and generosity to the matter at hand.

Read more about this novel and meet
the author at www.portobellobooks.com.
Here you'll find:

+ the inside story of how the novel was written

+ a guide for your reading group – complete with an author
interview and topics for discussion

+ the author's answers to the famous
Proust Questionnaire

+ a feature on the radio play of the novel

+ what it's like for a first-time author to become a
Commonwealth Prize winner

+ CS Richardson's recommendations for the all-time
great romantic movies

+ a Valentine's Day special: Portobello authors pick their most
romantic destination inspired by Ambrose Zephyr's list

+ a chance to win an advance copy of
CS Richardson's new novel

+

For news about current and forthcoming titles
from Portobello Books and for a sense of purpose
visit the website **www.portobellobooks.com**

Encouraging voices,
Supporting writers,
Challenging readers

Portobello
BOOKS